Disney · PIXAR

THE GOOD DINOSAUR

Wild Adventure

GOODDINO9228

Code is valid for your ebook and may be
redeemed through the Disney Story Central app
on the App Store. Content subject to availability.
Parent permission required.
Code expires on December 31, 2019.

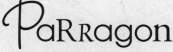

Bath · New York · Cologne · Melbourne · Delhi
Hong Kong · Shenzhen · Singapore · Amsterdam

Long ago, dinosaurs roamed the planet. One night, an asteroid blazed across the sky. It missed Earth, which meant that dinosaurs carried on living for thousands more years.

Meet Poppa, an Apatosaurus. He is very proud of the farm he and Momma have created.

This is Momma. She lives with Poppa on Clawtooth Mountain. They work hard on their farm to make sure there is enough food to eat.

Momma and Poppa decide to start a family.
They look on, excited and proud, as an egg is about to hatch.

The egg hatches open . . . it's a boy! Momma and Poppa name him Arlo. Little Arlo looks out at the bright world beyond his shell.

Arlo may be small, but he's happy. Some things scare him, though, like the world beyond the farm.

This is Arlo's brother, Buck. He is much stronger than Arlo.

Libby is Arlo's sister. She is much braver than Arlo.

Arlo does his best to keep up with his brother
and sister, but he still has a lot of growing up to do!

Arlo helps out on the family farm, too.
His job is to feed the animals.

But sometimes the family's animals scare Arlo . . .

. . . and sometimes he runs away!

All of the members of Arlo's family have made their mark on the food silo—except Arlo. He knows he'll have to do something big to earn his mark.

After a long, hard day at work, Poppa takes Arlo to a field on the farm. Suddenly, a firefly lands on Arlo's nose and scares him!

Poppa gently blows on the firefly
and it starts to glow, and Arlo feels safe.

The next day, Poppa gives Arlo an important task:
catching the critters who steal food from the silo.

Arlo catches a critter! He can earn his mark by getting rid of it, but his fear gets in the way and the critter escapes.

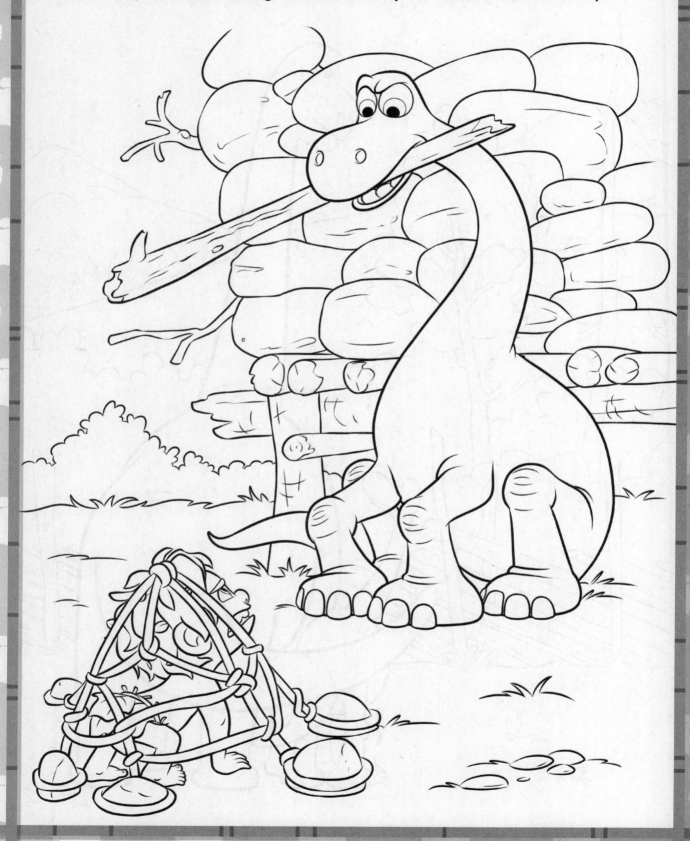

Poppa takes Arlo to the wilderness on the other side
of the fence to find the critter and face his fears.

Soon after, Arlo and Poppa get caught in a violent storm. Poppa pushes Arlo to safety, but then Poppa gets swept away in a flood and doesn't come back. . . .

Without Poppa, the family has to work twice as hard.
Arlo is desperate to help. He wants to prove that he, too,
deserves to make his mark on the silo.

But the family's hard work is for nothing.
Little creatures keep stealing their crops.
And this cute-looking critter is the main culprit!

One day, Arlo finds the little critter stealing corn!

The critter is curious. He jumps onto Arlo's snout and stares at him. Arlo freezes, slowly taking in the fearsome beast on his nose. . . .

Arlo and the critter fight over a piece of corn,
but they lose their balance and tumble into the river!

"ARGHHH!" The raging river swirls, carrying Arlo far, far away from his home and family.

Finally, Arlo is washed up on dry land.
He looks around to see if he can find his way home.
But all he can see is that crazy critter!

Arlo is angry with the
little critter—it has caused
him a lot of trouble!

The critter kicks dirt in Arlo's face and
runs into the wilderness. Arlo is not happy!

Arlo reaches a clifftop and looks down at the
valley far below him. Suddenly, he stops in his tracks.
"I can follow the river home!" Arlo realizes.

Arlo soon becomes very hungry.
He finds some berries high up
in a tree, but he can't reach them.

Arlo slips and falls trying to reach the berries,
and his foot gets stuck between some rocks.
Exhausted, he curls up for the night and falls asleep.

When Arlo wakes up, his foot is free! He sees some footprints in the mud. That little critter must have helped him.

Arlo continues on his way, but it starts to rain.
The little dinosaur decides to build a shelter.

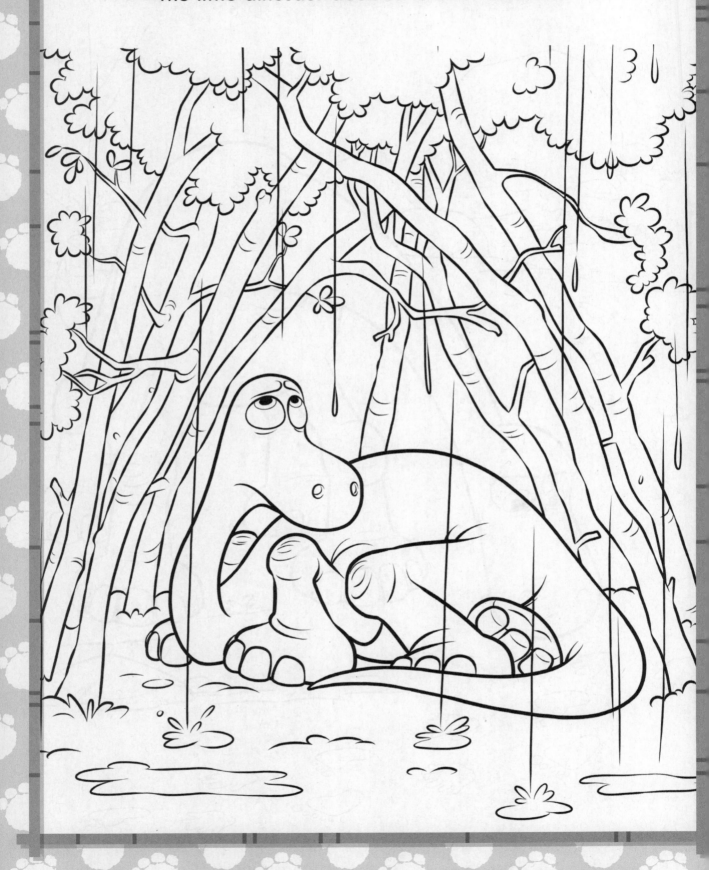

Arlo is frightened by the strange-looking
animals in the wilderness!

Suddenly, Arlo hears a rustling in the bushes. The critter runs toward Arlo and offers him some food—a lizard! Yuck! Arlo is not impressed.

The critter catches a bug for Arlo.
But Arlo doesn't like bugs much either. . . .

The critter brings Arlo some delicious berries. Arlo loves them!
They sit down together and munch away happily.

Arlo has a lot to learn about the wilderness.
The critter is a very good teacher!

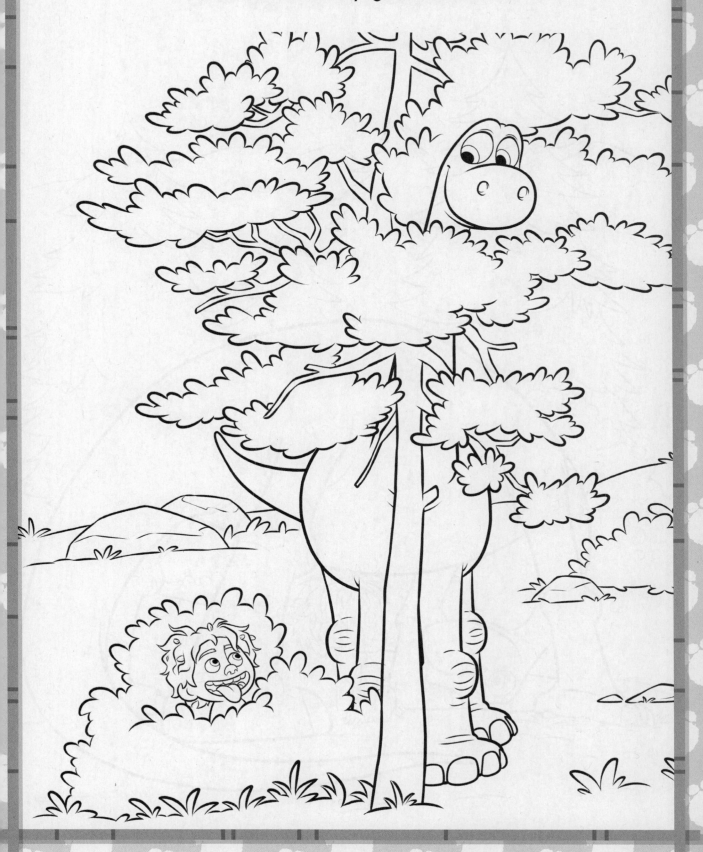

As they spend more time together,
Arlo and the little critter become friends.

A nervous Arlo
follows the critter
along a dangerous
path to look for
more berries.

Suddenly, a huge, scary snake ambushes them! The brave little critter leaps to defend his new friend.

Soon, the critter smells something in the bushes.
He sniffs around curiously, and then follows the trail.

The critter scratches to signal he has found something!

SQUEAK! SQUEAK! Lots of tiny gophers start
popping up out of the ground! Arlo and the critter
play a game with the gophers.

Later, Arlo meets a strange dinosaur named
Forrest Woodbush—who looks just like a tree!
Lots of animals like to hang out on Forrest's horns.

Forrest likes the critter and challenges Arlo to a naming contest: Whoever names the critter gets to keep him. "Spot!" says Arlo. The critter looks up. Arlo has won!

Forrest's pet bird, Debbie, gets mad.
She wants to keep Spot, too!

At night, hundreds of fireflies light up the sky. Arlo shows Spot how to play with them. The fireflies remind Arlo of his family.

Arlo uses twigs to tell Spot about his family. Spot starts making his own family out of twigs, too, but it makes him sad. He quickly covers up the two big twig people with dirt.

Spot and Arlo howl into the night,
remembering their families.

Spot rides on Arlo's back as
they continue their journey.

Arlo and Spot hear the rumble of thunder. A storm is approaching—fast! They run to find shelter in the forest.

Arlo and Spot hide under a tree root.
They look out timidly, waiting for the storm to pass.

After the storm, Arlo sees a flying Pterodactyl. Arlo hopes the Pterodactyl can show him and Spot the way home.

These Pterodactyls are storm chasers.
Their names are Coldfront, Thunderclap, and Downpour.

But the Pterodactyls are not so
friendly . . . they want to steal Spot!

Arlo is not about to let his new friend be taken by these storm chasers. He picks up Spot and runs away.

Just as they are making their escape, they run into a group of T. rexes! Luckily, the T. rexes are not as scary as they look. . . .

The T. rexes help fight off the Pterodactyls!

The first T. rex introduces himself as Nash.
He is happy to meet Arlo and Spot!

Ramsey is Nash's sister. Ramsey likes Spot!
She pets him and talks to him.

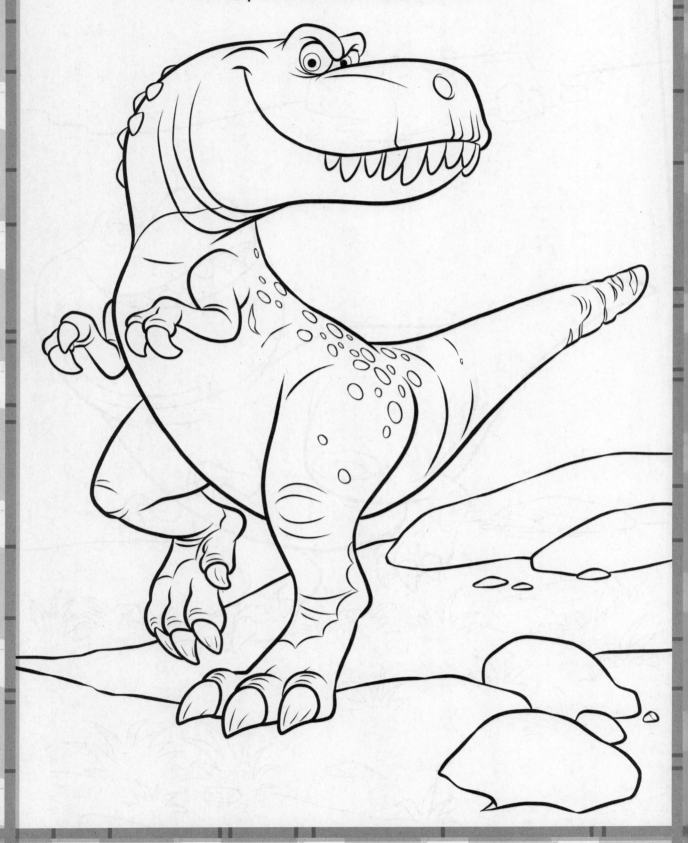

Spot smiles at Ramsey. "Well, ain't you just the cutest thing?" she says.

The biggest of the T. rexes is Butch. He is Nash and Ramsey's father. The T. rexes survive by herding longhorns, but they have lost their herd!

The two groups decide to help each other. Spot can sniff out anything, so Arlo's sure that Spot can find the lost longhorns!

The longhorns have been captured by rustlers. Butch has an idea: Arlo can help catch the rustlers by acting as bait!

Arlo is scared, but he's determined to help out his new friends. Arlo and Spot look for a place to attract the rustlers.

Spot bites Arlo, who lets out a huge yell! Spot hopes
the loud noise will bring the rustlers out of hiding.

The rustlers are mean-looking Raptors—
and they are ready to fight!

Butch, Nash, and Ramsey leap out of the grass and charge toward the Raptors.

Butch leads the charge. He corners one of the Raptors while Nash and Ramsey fight off the others.

Suddenly, the Raptors charge straight toward Arlo!
The little dinosaur is frozen in fear. But with Spot's
encouragement, he finds the courage to fight back.

Arlo, Spot, and the T. rexes fight off the Raptors together.
Arlo checks out his battle wounds with Spot by his side.

That night, Arlo and Spot join their new T. rex friends around a campfire. Nash plays the bug harmonica.

The three T. rexes tell stories about when they fought off other beasts. Ramsey shows off an old battle wound.

Once upon a time, Butch battled a crocodile! Its tooth is still in his cheek.

Snow begins to fall from the sky. Winter is coming!
Arlo knows it's time to get home to his Momma and the farm.

In the morning, Arlo and Spot help the T. rexes herd the longhorns.

Butch, Nash, and Ramsey show Arlo and Spot
the way to the river and then say their good-byes.
Spot and Arlo can see Clawtooth Mountain at last.

Spot and Arlo continue on their journey and follow the river toward Clawtooth Mountain.

The two friends play and laugh together as they stroll along. Soon, they come to the top of a hill.

Arlo pops his head through the clouds. What a view!
In the distance, they see Clawtooth Mountain.
They're almost home!

Soon, Spot sees a figure of a human in the distance.
Arlo is worried that Spot might leave him.

Suddenly, clouds start to gather and lightning flashes. A storm full of Pterodactyls appears in the sky!

Just then, Thunderclap the Pterodactyl
swoops down and captures Spot!

The Pterodactyls trap Spot inside a tree trunk
and circle him. Spot is in trouble! Until . . .

. . . brave Arlo shows up to rescue him! Arlo picks up a tree and throws it at the Pterodactyls with all his might. The creatures fly away, terrified.

Just then, a flash flood
comes rushing toward Spot.
Can Arlo reach him in time?

Just as the two friends reach each other,
they get swept over a waterfall!

Spot and Arlo get washed up on shore.
Arlo is grateful that Spot is okay!

The next morning, Spot and Arlo continue on their journey.
They see a human family near Clawtooth Mountain.
Spot crawls toward them, sniffing curiously.

The humans want to be Spot's new family.
Arlo is sad to see Spot go, but he knows it's for the best.
The two friends hug and say good-bye.

Soon after, Arlo finally sees his family's farm.
And he's no longer the little dinosaur he used to be. . . .

Arlo goes to the family silo and looks at the marks. At last, he can place his mark next to theirs.

Arlo has proven his strength and bravery.
He makes his mark on the silo with pride.

Momma, Buck, and Libby are so glad to have
Arlo back where he belongs. Arlo hugs his Momma.
He is happy to be home at last.